THE DAWN THREAD

A R Arnold

For those standing at the crossroads of midlife,
who carry the weight of what was,
and wonder what might still be.

For those searching beyond success, beyond
expectation,
for a life that feels their own.

May you find courage to untie old knots,
patience to weave new threads,
and faith that it is never too late
to begin again.

CONTENTS

Acknowledgement

Now you must ask, what thread will you weave with the time that remains?

THE DAWN TELLER

PROLOGUE

Elias was forty-seven years old, and he was tired.

Not the kind of tired that came from too little sleep or too much work. This was the heavier kind, the kind that settled into the bones and whispered in the quiet moments: *Is this it?*

He had spent two decades working in finance, climbing and slipping and climbing again, until at last the company's latest restructure took his position and his sense of identity with it. He had been given a handshake, a severance packet, and the kind of polite silence people offer when they don't know what else to say. For weeks he had carried that silence with him, along with the dull ache of purpose lost.

That night, he found himself in a dim bar at the edge of the city, nursing a drink he didn't particularly want. Around him, the world hummed with other people's laughter, but none of it seemed to reach him. He thought of his bills, his thinning hair, his daughter now living far away with the wife who had left years before. He thought of all the promises he had once made to himself, and how many of them had crumbled like old plaster.

He stepped outside for air. The alley was narrow, lined with wet cobblestones that glistened beneath a thin sliver of moon. He was about to turn back when he noticed it - light spilling through a cracked wooden door at the alley's end. Behind it drifted music, faint but alluring, like flutes played in a dream.

Elias hesitated. He thought he saw, just above the door, a streak of light cut across the sky - a falling star. He had not wished upon one since childhood, but something stirred in him. Quietly, without meaning to, he whispered: *I wish I could begin again. I wish I could learn how to live better than this.*

The door creaked open wider, as if it had been listening.

Drawn by a mix of weariness and curiosity, Elias stepped through. And in an instant, he was no longer in the alley but in a place alive with lanterns and voices. A marketplace stretched endlessly before him, strange and shimmering. Stalls overflowed with impossible things like bottled laughter, jars of silence, feathers of golden birds. It was at once foreign and familiar, like stepping into the pages of a forgotten story.

And so, his journey began.

THE DAWN THREAD

THE TIME MERCHANT

Elias stood with one hand extended into nothing, his fingers still remembering the rough grain of the cracked wooden door. He had pushed through it a heartbeat ago. Now there was only a wall, old brick veined with ivy, damp and ordinary in a way that felt unkind. The alley, the bar's neon smear, the throb of low music was now gone. No hinge. No handle. No way back.

He let his hand fall. The air here tasted of cinnamon and smoke.

Lanterns swung from iron hooks overhead, each flame a captive star. The marketplace unfolded in a maze of lanes and glowing stalls, a murmur of voices rising and falling in a dozen languages he did not know. Some merchants sang to the crowd; others sat unmoving, as if stillness itself were for sale. Shelves were stacked with even more impossible things: jars of silence that shivered if you breathed too close; cages whose shadows paced inside them like animals; feathers that shed gold dust, which refused to settle no matter how long he watched.

A child crouched on the cobbles near his boot, spinning a wooden top. The toy hummed and shivered, a thin circle of sound that threaded through the market's low roar. The child looked up with bright eyes, the lantern-light caught there like sparks.

"Where am I?" Elias asked. He heard the rasp in his own voice.

The child slowed the top with one fingertip, holding it quivering, then still. "Where you think you are," they said, with the contented certainty of someone who knows a secret and is not worried by it.

"That isn't an answer."

"It's the only answer." The child's mouth tilted in what might have been a smile. "For some, this is a market. For others, a dream. Some call it a trap. Some call it the beginning." A small shrug. "Everyone here is searching."

"For what?"

The child spun the top again. Its hum swelled until it was all he could hear. When the sound thinned, the child was gone. Only the toy remained, wobbling, then clattering to its side.

Elias looked back at the blank wall, one last, useless glance, and then moved forward. He drew his coat tighter. His palm still held the memory of damp wood. He followed the light.

The first stall he came to was quiet. Amid the cries of the market sellers - "Buy joy! Buy sleep! Buy courage!" - this one offered nothing but stillness. An old man sat behind a bare wooden table, his spine bent like a bow waiting to be strung. His hair was the color of ash; his eyes had the sharp, waiting gleam of clock hands. Before him, under the lantern's gold, stood a single hourglass. Its sand fell in a thin, indifferent stream.

"Welcome," the old man said. His voice was cracked but steady, like a dry riverbed after long rain. "I sell what no one else here can: time."

Elias let out a breath that was almost a laugh. "Time can't be bought."

The old man reached, and with two fingertips tilted the hourglass onto its side.

The sand froze. Each tiny fleck hung sparkling in the shaft of lantern light, a constellation caught midfall. In the sudden hush, the marketplace drew back as if a curtain had been tugged. The voices dimmed, footsteps softened, the smell of smoke thinned, and Elias could hear his own breathing, measured and unprepared.

Wonder struck him first, sharp as cold. Then something slower: a widening ache.

"Here," the old man said, sliding the glass toward

him, "everything is trade. Would you like another ten years? Fifteen? Enough to outlive your regrets, to finish what you did not begin, to mend what you let fray?"

The words made a space inside him, a hollowness quickly filled by pictures his mind summoned as if grateful to be asked.

He saw a conference room washed in winter light. The head of People & Culture, her careful voice, the mug in her hands she never drank from. *Restructuring. External conditions. Your contribution has been valued.* The way the word *valued* dropped between them without weight. Elias had stared at the snow of spreadsheets on the table, at a small chip in the edge of the laminate, and thought wildly of asking if he could fix the chip. He had signed papers. He had placed his lanyard, a simple plastic rectangle with his name and photo, into a tray that looked like an offering bowl. People had said they were sorry in voices that were not quite sorry, but more so relieved it wasn't them.

He saw, behind that, a porch on a late summer evening. His wife's hair pulled back, a glass of water sweating in her hand. Cicadas razoring the air. Her voice, soft and even the way a practiced musical note is even: *I can't keep doing this alone.* He had meant to argue, but the weight in her eyes had pressed the words flat. He had been at the office that night anyway, replying to emails that did not remember him now.

5

He saw his daughter, six years old, then twelve, then fifteen, receding from the door of a school auditorium where he arrived at the end of a song, holding flowers that felt foolish in his hands. *It's fine, Dad. Really.* The way she had smiled to make him feel better, learning too early the wrong kind of generosity.

"Ten years," Elias heard himself say, not as a decision but as a thought spoken aloud. The suspended sand glinted like a promise. "What's the price?"

The old man's smile was small and without triumph. "Memories. Not the painful ones. You may keep those if you like. Only the small joys. A child's laughter running across a yard. The warmth of a hand held in winter. Sleep ins on a morning when nothing is required of you. For each year you purchase, one such moment will vanish. You will not even know it is missing."

Elias's mouth went dry. Small joys. The phrase felt like a dismissal, and then immediately like a mercy he could not afford to lose. He thought of a Friday when his team stayed late and someone put a ridiculous song on, and they laughed so hard the glass walls shook with it. He thought of his daughter's socked feet sliding across a kitchen floor, her delight at the skid. He even thought of the morning after he was let go and how he walked out of the building to a sun he rarely saw, and how he drank his coffee slowly because, for the first time in a long time, he was in no rush to be anywhere.

The hourglass was cool when his fingertips found it, cool like stone at night. He wanted, he really wanted, to tip it upright and say *yes*. More time. A second chance. A chance to arrive early, to listen more than he defended, to refuse promotions with invisible chains. He could picture a future like a room filled with light into which he would step and become a better man just by crossing the threshold.

But another memory, thinner and truer, threaded through the want. He remembered sitting in a hospital waiting room while his father slept in a bed down the hall, a television bolted to the ceiling playing a show with the sound off. His father had woken and said, after a long, confusing minute, *It went fast, didn't it?* Elias had wanted to answer, *I wasn't watching,* and had not said it because it sounded cruel. But it was the truth. He had not been watching. He had been *busy*.

"If I didn't watch the time I had," he said, surprised to hear his own voice so low, "why would I watch the time I buy?"

The old man's eyes, which had been a metal gleam, softened. The slightest nod.

Elias's hand hovered. He had the wild thought that he could bargain: half years, cheaper moments for sale, a swap of certain griefs for certain joys. But the hourglass did not bargain. It lay on its side, a small universe arrested.

He pushed it gently back across the table.

"No," he said. The word was not firm, but it held.

The old man set the glass upright. The grains loosened, then poured. Sound returned: shoes on stone, a low call, a clink of something metal. The lantern's light seemed warmer.

"Wise," the old man murmured. There was no victory in it. "Remember: time cannot be owned, only lived. Those who buy years discover that emptiness is expensive."

Elias drew a breath. It went deeper than the breaths he had been taking. He stepped away, but only a pace, and looked again at the hourglass. The stream of sand was the same as it had been when he first saw it, and not the same at all.

He turned and found the marketplace had crept closer. People brushed past; men in coats too heavy for the warmth, women with baskets slung from their shoulders, a figure in a cloak whose edges smoked and then were only fabric again. A vendor somewhere snapped a cloth in the air and laughter burst like a flock.

He took one step, then another. He had the feeling, clear and unsettling, that the choice he had made was a door, and that by passing through it he had locked it behind him. He was tempted to look back at the wall again but did not. The wall would be there whether he looked or not. There was only forward.

As he walked, the market echoed him back to himself. A ribbon of gold dust along a stall's edge reminded him of his daughter when she was three, how she had insisted on sprinkling glitter onto a birthday card until it poured off the table like sand. A bell chimed somewhere, two notes, and he remembered the small kitchen timer his wife used, the ding that meant the cake was done, the way she would touch the top with one finger and smile without looking up. The past came not as an accusation but as proof that it had been real.

He touched his coat pocket and was surprised to find nothing there. He had the urge to take something from the stall, a token to make the lesson stay. But the old man had given him nothing, and that seemed right. Not everything you keep is something you can hold.

At the edge of the next lane he paused and looked back once, not at the wall but at the quiet stall. The old man had already turned to another passerby, his hand making its small, precise gesture. Elias could not hear their words, but he knew their gravity. He felt, in his own chest, the pull of *yes* and the weight of *no*.

He stepped into the new lane. The air cooled. The light changed. Somewhere ahead, a bright clatter of coins rose and fell like sea on rock. He found that he was listening differently, listening to the space between sounds, to the way the market breathed. The child's words curled back to him: *For some, a trap. For others, the beginning.*

He did not know which he had walked into yet. He only knew that time had resumed, and that he could feel it now, not as an enemy or a vanishing resource, but as a living thing moving beside him. Each grain falling. Each one unrepeatable.

He slowed his pace, just enough to notice. He would carry that with him, if he could, into whatever waited next.

THE MONEY CHANGER

The lane bent toward brightness. Elias could hear it before he saw it, a shimmer in the air, like the sound of coins tumbling endlessly. The air here smelled of leather and smoke, sharper than before, as though a furnace burned behind the walls.

Where the Time Merchant's stall had been bare, this one blazed with opulence. Coins spilled in shining cascades across a polished table. Chains of gold and silver draped from hooks, heavy and beautiful. Gems pulsed faintly as though alive, breathing in their own light. Parchments lay stacked in neat towers, their ink smoking and rearranging itself into words Elias almost recognized.

The man behind the stall was tall, his robe a midnight fabric embroidered with silver threads that moved like water. His smile was wide, deliberate, the kind of smile Elias remembered from men in expensive suits, those colleagues who had outpaced him, executives who shook hands too firmly, bankers who promised safety in return for surrender.

"Ah," the man said, his voice polished smooth. "At last, a customer who understands value. Come closer."

Elias felt his chest tighten. The scene was painfully familiar. The stall smelled of ambition, of boardrooms with dark wood tables, of cigars and aftershave, of late nights when deals were struck under fluorescent light. He remembered those years, how hard he had worked, how often he had gone home long after his wife and daughter were asleep. He remembered telling himself it was temporary, that all of it was *for them*.

"What do you sell?" he asked.

The merchant gestured at the wealth spread across the table. "Freedom from worry. Prosperity. The life you deserved but never claimed." He leaned forward, his silver-threaded sleeves whispering across the wood. "I offer you abundance, Elias. Enough to buy back your pride, your comfort, your legacy."

Elias's breath caught. The man had spoken his name. He hadn't given it.

The merchant raised one hand. The air rippled like water, and before Elias's eyes a vision unfolded.

He stood in a house by the sea, glass walls open to an endless horizon. Light streamed through every room. His daughter's laughter rang out, not the shy smile she gave him now, but the pure, open laughter of a girl who trusted. She sat at a grand piano, playing clumsy chords, looking at him with pride. His wife was there too, her hand warm in his, her eyes soft, as though the years of distance had never carved their space.

Elias's throat ached. He wanted to step forward into that vision, to live inside it. He wanted it more than breath.

"You see?" the Money Changer said softly. "This is what was always meant for you. All you need to do is claim it."

The parchments stirred. One unrolled itself, curling flat on the table. The ink shimmered, alive. Elias read the words forming:

In exchange for wealth unending, the bearer offers...

Beneath, three choices glowed: Health. Integrity. Joy.

His fingers twitched. His health already faltered from years of stress, the knots in his back tightened, and the exhaustion he never quite shook. Could he give it up for this? Integrity? He saw himself agreeing to decisions he despised, twisting truth, shaking hands he did not trust. Joy? He saw laughter drain from his days, replaced by long nights staring at ceilings, wealth piled in corners while his spirit withered. Maybe trading one of them wasn't a loss at all.

The merchant leaned closer, his voice like velvet. "Think, Elias. No more hunger for respect. No more scraping. No more shame when you walk into a room and feel yourself smaller. With wealth, you will be seen. You will be remembered. Your daughter will never pity you again."

Elias's hand hovered above the parchment. Heat rose from the ink, a pulsing that seemed to draw him in. His chest hammered. He thought of promotions lost, of men younger than him leaping ahead while he stayed, steady but overlooked. He thought of walking home past glass towers still glowing, each window another desk where someone richer and more powerful sealed their future. He thought of the nights his wife had begged him to come home early, and he had stayed anyway, chasing figures on a screen.

The vision shimmered brighter. His wife's hand, warm in his. His daughter's laughter. A home that welcomed him instead of resenting his absence.

His hand trembled. He could sign. He could *fix it all.*

Then another memory cut through, sharp as glass. The Time Merchant's voice: *Time cannot be owned, only lived.*

Elias blinked. The vision flickered. The mansion dimmed. His wife's hand grew cold, slipping into smoke. His daughter's eyes hardened, not soft with pride but heavy with expectation. Around him, the gold chains shimmered, and for a moment he saw the truth: each contract was a shackle. Each gem a weight. Each buyer a prisoner.

He saw the others crowded at the stall, a woman clutching a ruby necklace, her hands shaking under its weight. A man signing his name in burning ink, golden cuffs locking around his wrists. They smiled, yes, but their eyes were hollow.

Elias pulled his hand back. His breath shook. "No."

The merchant's smile faltered. "You refuse?"

"I do." Elias swallowed. "I've already paid enough. I won't pay again."

The parchment curled in on itself, smoking back into nothing. The jewels dimmed. The coins seemed duller, their glow gone. The merchant's smile returned, but now it was brittle, sharp at the edges.

"Few walk away," he said. "Most are eager to trade."

Elias turned from the stall, his legs unsteady, but his chest strangely lighter. He could still taste the salt air of the vision, still hear the laughter that wasn't real. He had told himself *no* but the echo of *yes* still tugged at him.

He paused.

Behind him the coins clinked, the parchment whispered, and for a heartbeat he felt it again: the pull of the mansion by the sea, the hand in his, the look of pride in his daughter's eyes. His body swayed as though drawn back, as though the vision might still open if he reached for it.

The merchant's smile widened, sensing his hesitation. He slid a parchment toward Elias, slow as a predator. The ink shimmered invitingly, the words forming again: *In exchange for wealth unending...*

And then Elias saw them.

They hung just beyond the table, glimmering faintly in the lantern light, handcuffs wrought of pure gold, polished so bright they seemed like jewelry. For an instant they looked beautiful. Then he noticed the bruises on the wrists of those who wore them, the way the metal bit deep, leaving marks that no wealth could cover. The chains were heavy, though the wearers smiled. Their laughter was hollow, the sound of people pretending not to hear their own shackles.

The sight struck Elias harder than the vision of the mansion. He staggered back as if scorched. The glow of the gold pressed against him, dazzling, suffocating. He shrank away from it, not into shadow like a vampire fleeing light, but into the relief of shadow, as though the glare of false brilliance might burn him alive.

"No," he whispered again, more fiercely this time. "No."

The merchant's smile cracked, sharp and thin. The parchment curled into smoke, the jewels dulled, the golden handcuffs vanished into darkness.

Elias turned, his steps quick now, almost a retreat. Behind him the clatter of coins rose and fell like a tide that would never stop. Ahead, the marketplace grew dimmer, quieter, the light softening into shadow. He pressed forward, carrying with him not the promise of riches but the certainty of their chains.

THE MIRROR SELLER

The marketplace narrowed into a quieter street where the lanterns hung lower and the light turned pale, like dawn that never fully arrived. The air was cooler here, carrying a faint metallic tang that reminded Elias of blood on his tongue after biting it. Voices hushed, footsteps softened. It felt less like a market and more like a cathedral of shadows.

Elias walked slowly, unsettled by the silence. He still carried the echo of the Money Changer's stall in his chest with the salt air of the vision, the warmth of his wife's hand, his daughter's laughter in a house that never was. And beneath it, the weight of the Time Merchant's warning: *time cannot be owned, only lived.*

The lane widened suddenly. Before him stood a stall that was no stall at all but a wall of mirrors.

They leaned against one another in uneasy angles, their frames carved of bone, wood, and silver.

Some gleamed so bright they seemed like doorways. Others swirled as though fog pressed against the glass. The air hummed faintly, not with sound but with vibration, as if the mirrors themselves breathed.

A woman emerged from the shadows behind them, her robe a shifting gauze that seemed woven from mist. Her eyes were pale, nearly colorless, but their gaze was relentless, stripping Elias bare.

"Welcome," she said, her voice low and resonant. "Here you will see the lives you did not choose. The ones that still live behind you."

Elias's stomach turned, but his feet carried him closer. One mirror caught his eye. He froze.

In it, a younger Elias grinned, his arm wrapped around a girl he had once loved fiercely before he met his wife. They stood in a kitchen of their own, sunlight pouring through the window, her laughter as familiar as a song he had not heard in decades. In that life, he had never walked away. He had married her. Built something different. The love glowed easy and bright, untouched by the years of tension that had eaten his real marriage.

His chest ached. *If only I had stayed.*

Then the truth pierced him: in that mirror, his daughter did not exist. He searched, frantic, but the girl he knew was nowhere in that life. The warmth of this vision was paid for by her absence.

He staggered back. Another mirror seized him.

There he stood in a boardroom, older but powerful, a man risen high. His colleagues leaned forward when he spoke, his words commanding. His wife sat at his side at dinners, proud, radiant. His daughter worked beside him, sharp and ambitious, her eyes shining with approval.

Pride surged in him. He could almost feel the respect, the recognition he had hungered for all his life.

But the reflection flickered. His wife's smile faltered, her eyes dimming with fatigue. His daughter's ambition hardened her face into his own mask, her laughter gone. The empire of his success had stolen something gentler from them both.

He tore his gaze away, but another mirror caught him.

Here he was younger still, twenty, a backpack slung across his shoulders, the world unrolling before him. He had never taken the safe job. He had travelled instead, wandered, tasted freedom. His eyes gleamed with a wild spark, free of exhaustion. Around him were mountains, seas, the endless road.

Elias's throat tightened with longing. He had once dreamed of this. He had once believed he could live that way. He pressed his forehead to the glass. *If only I had been braver.*

The mirror shivered, and the scene shifted. He sat

alone by a fire in some remote place, the mountains beautiful but indifferent. No wife. No daughter. No one to carry his stories home. Freedom had cost him belonging.

He spun, desperate, but every mirror showed him something else: a life as a writer, pages scattered around a desk, but no family to distract him from his words; a life as a musician on a stage, adored but hollow, the applause fading into silence each night; a life where his marriage had endured, but it had endured like a house patched with rotten wood, full of silence instead of shouting, together but not alive.

Each mirror glowed with promise. Each revealed its hidden shadow.

The Mirror Seller's voice wove around him. "So many doors left unopened. Each choice you did not take still breathes behind you. Do you not long to step through, to claim what you lost?"

Elias's whole body trembled. His youth haunted him now, more than the wealth he had refused, more than the time he had declined to buy. Youth with its open doors, its bright potential, had slipped through his fingers, stolen by years, by choices, by responsibilities he had carried until they bent his shoulders. He felt a deep melancholy, a mourning for the boy he had been and for the man he might have become.

"Yes," he whispered. The word tore from his chest. "God, yes."

The nearest mirror rippled like water. Its surface

softened, inviting. He could step through. He could choose again.

His hand lifted. The glass was cool beneath his palm, pliant, like the skin of a lake at dusk. The reflection reached toward him, smiling with promise.

Then, a twist. The laughter of his alternate daughter stilled. The proud smile of his wife in the boardroom collapsed into weariness. The traveler by the fire shivered in his solitude.

Elias's heart stopped. He saw it clearly now: every choice cost all others. To take one path was to burn the rest. To step into that mirror was not to gain, but to lose everything else. The butterfly's wings beat, and the storm erased every life but the one chosen.

The Mirror Seller's pale eyes locked onto his. "Regret is endless," she said softly. "The past can be seen, but not lived twice. Each *if only* hides a *but then.*"

Elias's hand dropped. His knees felt weak, but his chest swelled with something fierce - grief, yes, but also clarity.

He looked once more at the mirrors. They showed him now as he was, his current self: weary, lined, imperfect. But real. Alive. Him.

"I won't step through," he said.

The mirrors darkened, one by one, until only their glassy silence remained.

The Mirror Seller inclined her head, her gauze shifting like fog. "Then walk on, Elias. And remember:

youth passes, choices close, doors seal. But there is still one door that remains open and that is the one before you now."

Elias turned, stumbling a little as he left the stall. The ache of lost youth pressed heavy on him, but he carried with it a new understanding: longing for the past only sharpened the loss of the present.

The marketplace awaited him, another lesson stirring in its depths.

THE WEIGHT KEEPER

The lane from the mirrors narrowed into shadow, as though the market itself meant for him to walk more slowly. Elias's chest still ached from what he had seen - all those lives he had not lived, all those doors closed forever. His youth had slipped away, taken by time and choices, and he felt the melancholy of it heavy in his bones.

Yet as he moved forward, he noticed something strange: though he had stepped away from the mirrors, he carried their weight with him. Regret clung like a stone in his pocket. His shoulders sagged. His steps dragged.

He came into a square. At its center stood a stall piled high with bundles. Some were small as books, wrapped in twine. Others were as large as trunks, their ropes fraying under strain. They were stacked in precarious towers, leaning against one another, groaning softly as if alive.

Behind them sat a woman with arms thick as branches and eyes that burned like coals. She was neither young nor old, but carved from something older than both. When she spoke, her voice carried the weight of stone dragged across stone.

"Welcome, Elias," she said. "Here lies what you carry. Every burden. Every promise. Every failure you refused to put down."

Elias's eyes widened. He felt it immediately. Recognition. The bundles called to him. He stepped closer, his heart pounding, and saw names scrawled faintly across the cloth: *Work. Marriage. Fatherhood. Debt. Regret. Guilt. Hope.*

His breath caught. He reached for one marked *Fatherhood.* It was smaller than he expected, but heavier than any he had lifted before. He staggered under its pull, remembering late nights he had missed, promises he had broken. The weight was not only responsibility but guilt with the heaviness of what he had not done.

Another bundle caught his eye. *Marriage.* He touched it and felt the silence of his porch, the soft *I can't do this alone.* The burden throbbed with what he had lost, what he had let slip through his fingers.

He turned to *Work.* That bundle was jagged, cutting into his palms. It smelled of paper and ink and endless fluorescent light. He dropped it quickly, his hands trembling.

Elias's knees buckled. His whole life was here,

wrapped and bound, and he had dragged it with him without knowing.

The Weight Keeper leaned forward. "You cannot carry all of it. Few men can. Some break. Some are buried. You must choose."

Elias looked up, sweat beading on his brow. "How do I know which to keep?"

Her coal-dark eyes softened. "Ask yourself which burdens shape you, and which only break you. Not all weight is yours. Not all guilt belongs in your pack."

Temptation seized him then. He wanted to lay it all down, every stone, every rope, every load. To walk away empty, lighter than air, untethered. The vision swelled in his mind: himself free, roaming without duty, without expectation.

He staggered back, dizzy with desire.

But then another vision flickered, that of a man without ties, wandering with nothing in his hands. No daughter to anchor him, no memories to steady him, no promises to make him strong. Freedom without weight left him hollow, a shadow drifting without shape.

Elias sank to his knees before the bundles. He reached again for *Fatherhood.* It was heavy, but he held it. He would not lay it down. He reached for *Hope* too, surprised by its weight but unwilling to leave it behind.

But *Work*, no, he set it gently on the ground. That bundle no longer served him. *Debt* too, though sticky in his grip, he loosened and placed aside. He let go of *Regret,* though it clung like tar, pulling strands from him as it fell. His arms shook, but his chest lifted when it left him.

When he stood again, his shoulders felt lighter. Still burdened, yes, but not crushed.

The Weight Keeper nodded slowly, as if this choice had been made not here but long ago, and only now acknowledged. "Good," she said. "Strength is not in carrying everything, Elias. It is in knowing what to carry, and what to set down."

Elias bowed his head. His breath came easier, deeper. For the first time since entering the marketplace, he felt as though he was walking not only forward but upward, each step less heavy than the one before.

As he turned from the stall, the bundles behind him groaned and shifted, already reshaping themselves for the next weary soul who would come.

He moved back into the marketplace, the lanterns flaring brighter as if in recognition. Somewhere ahead, another lesson waited. But this time, Elias did not dread it.

He carried less. And what he carried, he carried with purpose.

THE COMPASS STALL

The marketplace hushed as Elias walked. The noise of bargaining, the glitter of coins, even the groan of burdens faded into silence. The air here was different. It felt cleaner, cooler, carrying the faint smell of rain. Lanterns swayed above, their flames steady.

He felt lighter than before, but also strangely hollow. He had set down burdens, turned away from regret, rejected wealth and false time. But he carried no direction. He realised, with a sting, that his life had been built on goals he had not chosen for himself, but he had no idea what else there could be.

At the end of the lane, a small stall stood waiting. On its table, resting on a square of velvet, lay a single compass. Its brass was dented and worn, its glass scratched. Yet the needle spun furiously, rattling against the glass as if trapped.

Behind the table sat an old woman, her hair white, her eyes kind and piercing all at once.

"Welcome," she said. "Tell me, where are you going?"

Elias swallowed. "I don't know."

She nodded once, as if this was the only answer he could give. "Pick it up."

He did. The compass was warm, heavier than it looked. The needle spun, frantic, refusing to rest.

"It won't settle," Elias said.

"Not until you know what you value," the woman replied.

He frowned. "I do know."

"Do you? Speak it."

He paused, thinking of the market sellers he had just seen and wondering if, in fact, he did know. What he did know is what he had always known, what his whole life had been about, so he straightened, as though sitting in a boardroom again, and tried. "Success."

The needle spun faster.

"Security."

The rattling grew louder.

"Wealth. Recognition."

The needle whirled so wildly it blurred, desperate, as though trying to break free.

Elias's chest tightened. These had been the pillars of his life, his father's words, his mother's quiet pride when he brought home good marks, the way his father's friends had admired his business acumen. His father had been a man of stature, known in the community, respected. Elias had grown in that shadow, measuring himself against it every day. To succeed was to be his father's son. To fail was to be no one at all.

He thought of his friends too, men who seemed to glide through life. One with a flourishing career and a smiling family in photos. Another with a beach house, every summer documented in glossy frames. Elias had sat at dinner tables with them, nodding, smiling, swallowing envy like bile. He had believed they had what he lacked: control, composure, *the secret*. He had built his life in comparison, chasing their image as if it could fill him.

But standing here, with the compass spinning madly in his hand, he felt it all collapse. Success, security, wealth, recognition, none of them could steady the needle. They had only spun him in circles, his entire life chasing a north that wasn't his own.

His throat tightened. "If not these... then what?" His voice broke. "This is all I've ever known."

The old woman leaned forward. She placed one hand over the compass, stilling its spin for a moment. Then she drew her hand away, leaving the circle blank.

"Fill it," she said gently. "Not with what was given to you. Not with what others demand. Speak what is yours."

Elias stared at the empty space. His chest felt hollowed out, stripped bare. But into that emptiness rose something fragile, small but stubborn.

He thought of his daughter, laughing as she slid across the kitchen floor. Not success. Not wealth. Just her joy, spilling into his heart.

"Love," he whispered.

The needle slowed.

He thought of mornings when he sat with a cup of coffee and the quiet, the way peace felt like a gift he had never paid for.

"Peace."

The needle steadied further.

He thought of freedom, the freedom to be himself, unmasked, unshackled by others' expectations.

"Freedom."

The needle stopped. Firm. North.

Elias's breath left him in a rush. The compass glowed faintly in his palm, warm as if alive. His eyes stung.

The old woman smiled. "There. Your true north. Not your father's. Not your friends'. Yours. Love. Peace. Freedom."

Grief washed through him, grief for wasted years chasing false stars, for youth spent in comparison, for the weight of a legacy that was never truly his. But with it came relief. He had been spinning for decades. At last, the compass was still.

"Keep it," the woman said. "It will not tell you where to go. Only who you are."

Elias closed his hand around the compass. When he turned to walk, the lanterns ahead flared brighter. He felt sorrow still, but now it was sorrow with direction, and that was something like hope.

THE PASSION WEAVER

The compass lay warm in Elias's pocket, steady now. For the first time since stepping into the market-place, he walked with something like purpose. Yet still, doubt lingered at the edges of his mind. A compass could show direction but it could not tell him *how* to walk. Or *why*.

The marketplace opened into a courtyard bathed in shifting colors. Fabrics stretched overhead like sails, woven in every shade imaginable: scarlet, indigo, green, gold. They swayed gently as if stirred by an invisible hand, and with each ripple they changed, new patterns blooming across their surfaces before fading again. The air smelled of dye and smoke, rich and strange.

At the center of the courtyard sat a woman before a loom. Her hands moved swiftly, threading strands of light instead of thread. With every pass of the shuttle, the fabric on her loom shimmered with scenes of mountains, rivers, fires, and faces woven together in dazzling detail.

Elias stopped, entranced.

The woman looked up. Her eyes were bright as polished glass, alive with quiet fire. "Welcome, Elias. You have laid down burdens, faced your regrets, and found your compass. Now you must ask, what thread will you weave with the time that remains?"

Elias hesitated. His mouth went dry. "I don't know."

"You once did," she said gently. She gestured to the loom. The fabric shifted, and Elias gasped.

The woven image showed him as a boy, sprawled on the floor with pencils and paper, sketching endlessly, images of creatures, machines, maps of worlds that did not exist. His father's voice echoed faintly: *Art is no future. You need something solid, respectable.* The boy in the tapestry lowered his head, pushed the paper aside, and opened a math book.

Another image bloomed: Elias in his twenties, hunched over a guitar in a cramped flat. Music spilled from him, awkward but alive. His friends laughed and sang along. The room was thick with smoke and hope. Then the scene shifted: the guitar stored in a case beneath a bed, dust gathering while he typed late into the night, chasing promotions.

A third image shimmered: Elias speaking animatedly in a classroom. His daughter sat among other children, eyes wide as he explained something simple, the thrill of sharing knowledge lighting his face. But the image faded, and in its place he saw himself years later, declining her request to help with homework. *I'm busy. Ask your mother.*

Elias's chest ached. "I remember these," he whispered. "I loved them. But life..." He gestured helplessly. "Life pulled me away."

The woman's hands did not stop moving. "Passion is never lost, Elias. Only left unwoven. The strands are still here." She held up threads of color: red, blue, and gold. "But you must choose. Which threads will you pick up again? And which will you let remain loose?"

Elias reached out. The red thread pulsed warmly. He thought of his sketches, the joy of making something from nothing. "Art," he said softly.

The blue thread glimmered, humming with memory. He thought of his guitar, the way music made the air vibrate like shared breath. "Music."

The gold thread shone bright. He thought of the joy in his daughter's eyes when he explained something to her, the thrill of connection. "Teaching."

The loom hummed as each thread wove itself into the fabric. For a moment, Elias saw a vision: himself older, perhaps grayer, but alive with these passions, giving, creating, sharing. His chest swelled with possibility.

Then another thread caught his eye, black, heavy, almost sticky. He touched it and shuddered. The loom filled with images of late nights at the office, empty desks, glowing screens, endless numbers. "Work," he muttered. The thread felt dead in his hand. He let it fall.

The woman's eyes softened. "Good. Not all threads must be woven. Some weigh the fabric down until nothing shines through."

Elias felt tears sting his eyes. He had lived half a life convinced passion was for the young, that midlife was too late. But here, the strands still waited, vibrant as ever. He could choose them now, and the fabric of his days would be different.

He looked at the woman. "Is it too late to weave a new pattern?"

Her hands slowed on the loom. "The cloth is not finished, Elias. It never is until the end. Every choice is a new stitch. Every day, a thread. Midway is not the end. It is the moment you see the design clearly for the first time."

Elias pressed a hand to his pocket where the compass lay. He felt its steady pull, aligned now with threads he thought he had lost. Love, peace, freedom woven together with art, music, teaching. A life not rich in wealth, but in meaning.

The woman lifted the shimmering fabric from her loom. For an instant, Elias saw himself within it, flawed but whole, stitched from past and future both. Then the vision folded, dissolving into air.

"Go," she said, smiling. "And weave wisely."

Elias bowed his head. His throat was tight, but his chest felt alive in a way it had not for decades. As he walked from the courtyard, colors swayed overhead like banners, and the scent of dye clung to his coat as if to remind him: the strands of passion were his to claim, still waiting, still alive.

THE BLIND BEGGAR

The colors of the Passion Weaver's courtyard still shimmered in Elias's mind, the red for art, blue for music, and gold for teaching. For the first time in years, he felt his chest swell with possibility. Yet even as the warmth lingered, a shadow crept in.

How many times have I felt this before? he asked himself. *How many times have I promised myself that I would change, only to slip back into the same grooves within days?*

He remembered New Year's resolutions scribbled in notebooks, gym memberships paid for but abandoned, vows to spend more time with his family that dissolved into late nights at the office. He remembered how good intentions had always felt like strong winds, carrying him forward for a time until the calm came, and he settled back into the old ruts.

The more he thought on it, the heavier the realization became. What good were passions rediscovered if his habits dragged him back to the same hollow places?

The marketplace lane narrowed, the noise thinning until silence pressed around him. There, slumped against the wall of a shuttered stall, sat a man. His clothes were torn, his hair matted, and his eyes clouded white. A wooden bowl rested at his feet, empty.

"Spare a coin?" the beggar asked. His voice was calm, neither pleading nor bitter, but carrying a weight that made Elias pause.

Elias patted his pockets, but they were empty. "I have nothing to give."

The beggar tilted his head. "Then give me what costs you nothing, your ears."

Elias lowered himself onto the cobblestones.

The beggar's sightless eyes turned toward him. "Do you know why I am blind?"

Elias hesitated. "Illness? Old age?"

A thin smile ghosted across the man's lips. "No. I walked the same path every day until its walls grew so high I could no longer see over them. Blindness is not always in the eyes. It is in the doing."

Elias frowned. "Habits," he murmured.

"Ah," the beggar said, nodding. "Now you see. Habits are the grooves we carve into the earth. You think you live by choice, but you live by pattern. Walk the same path long enough, and it becomes the only way you know."

With a finger worn and scarred, the beggar traced two lines in the dust. One was deep, gouged firmly into the ground. The other was faint, a shallow scratch.

"This line," he said, pointing to the deeper one, "is the path you already walk. It is the habit formed by repetition. It is comfortable, familiar, easy to follow. Each day you walk it, the trench grows deeper, until you cannot climb its walls."

His finger moved to the faint scratch. "This line is the one you say you want. It is the new path. At first it is shallow, fragile. But if you step into it, day after day, the groove deepens. Soon it becomes stronger than the old. This is how lives change: one step repeated, until the earth remembers."

Elias stared at the lines. Simple scratches in dust, yet they cut into him like a blade. He thought of the ruts he had carved for himself: the ritual of late nights at work, the reach for a drink when the silence grew heavy, the endless scrolling through news and noise instead of picking up a pen.

He whispered, "I have lived in trenches."

The beggar tilted his head. "And you will stay there, unless you learn to climb."

From beneath his ragged shirt, the beggar drew out a length of rope. It was knotted crudely, each knot thick and uneven, the whole piece twisted into a loop like a necklace. He held it out.

"Here. This is habit," he said. "Each knot is a choice repeated until it hardens. Put it around your neck."

Elias hesitated. "Why a necklace?"

"Because habits are as close as breath," the beggar said. "They go where you go. They rest against your skin. And if they are left to grow without care, they do not rest, they choke."

Elias slipped the rope over his head. It settled heavy on his chest, the knots pressing into his skin. For a moment, he swore he felt it tighten, constricting his throat.

He clawed at it instinctively. "It feels... suffocating."

The beggar nodded. "So do bad habits. They take without asking, binding tighter with each repetition. One day you wake, and you no longer breathe freely. You are carried by them, not the other way around."

Elias ran a trembling hand over the knots. Each felt like years of repetition, hardened choices he no longer even remembered making. He thought of evenings when he promised change but returned to old patterns, blind and bound.

His voice cracked. "And how do I untie them?"

"Slowly," the beggar said. "Patience is the only knife that cuts these knots. Untie one, and tie another in its place - one that serves, not strangles. Habits do not vanish. They are replaced. Each new knot is a pattern of your choosing."

The beggar leaned closer, his voice almost a whisper. "Do not wait for great changes. Begin with small ones. Walk the shallow line until it grows deep. Tie a single good knot until it holds. Habits are blind, but they are faithful. Train them, and even in your weakest moments, they will carry you."

The rope felt heavy, but Elias understood its weight now. It was not a punishment, but a reminder. His future would not be built by dreams or regrets, but by the daily knots he tied and the paths he chose to walk.

He bowed his head. "Thank you."

The beggar's smile deepened. "Do not thank me. Thank the day. Each one is another chance to begin again."

The breeze shifted. When Elias looked up, the beggar was gone, leaving only silence and the necklace on his chest. The knots pressed gently against his throat, not choking, but reminding.

He rose slowly, the rope heavy yet grounding. Ahead, lanterns flickered, and faces gleamed in the shadows, waiting. Elias touched the rope, steadying himself. Habits would not vanish in a single moment but now he knew how to walk differently.

And he knew that if he forgot, the knots at his throat would remind him.

THE MASK MAKER

The marketplace narrowed again, the lanterns here dim and low, their flames flickering as though starved of air. Shadows pooled thick along the walls, swallowing sound. Elias's hand strayed to the knotted rope that lay against his chest. The rough loops pressed into his skin, each knot a reminder of choices repeated until they hardened. He felt its weight as he walked, grounding him. The air smelled faintly of wax and paint, a sharp artificial tang that made him think of old theaters, places where people performed roles that were never truly theirs.

He turned a corner and stopped.

Before him was a stall crowded with faces.

Dozens , even hundreds of masks stared back at him. They hung in neat rows from ropes overhead, lined shelves like jars in a pantry, and covered the table in chaotic piles. Some were crude, carved from wood, their features flat and stern. Others were painted in vivid colors, laughing, crying, sneering. A few were gilded, set with jewels, shining too brightly to look at for long.

Behind the stall stood a tall figure cloaked in black. Their face was hidden by a plain white mask, blank except for the faint outline of eyes. When they spoke, the voice was soft but carried strangely, as though it came from behind a wall.

"Welcome, Elias. You've laid down burdens, faced regret, found your compass, and chosen your threads of passion. But tell me, whose life are you weaving? Your own? Or the one others demanded of you?"

Elias's stomach tightened. His learning had shown him that he had to choose his own values, to be true to himself, but he was still many things to many people and his identity was sewn into that fabric as well as his own. His eyes moved across the masks, and his breath caught.

One mask shone like polished silver, sharp-jawed and confident. It was the mask of *The Successful Man*. He had worn it for decades, in boardrooms and interviews, dinners with colleagues, even around his own family. He lifted it, placed it over his face.

The world sharpened instantly. He felt taller, stronger. He imagined his father looking at him, nodding with pride: *That's my son. He made it.* He imagined his friends, their envy and admiration.

But beneath the mask, his chest ached. The edges pressed hard into his skin, muffling his breath. He remembered nights spent at the office, the way his wife's voice had trembled when she said she couldn't keep doing it alone. He remembered his daughter's tired smile when he arrived late, again. Success had been a mask, and behind it, he had been shrinking. The necklace tightened at his throat. The knots pressed hard into his skin, cutting his breath. He clawed at the rope, gasping. The mask's vision faltered, and beneath it he felt not admiration but suffocation. With a cry, he tore it off. The rope loosened, air rushing back into his lungs.

The Mask Maker tilted their head. "Comfortable, wasn't it? Until it choked you."

Next, his hand found the mask of *The Perfect Father*. Its mouth was carved in a permanent smile, its eyes gentle, endlessly patient. He slipped it on. A glow of approval washed over him. People admired him, respected him, praised him as a man who "always put family first."

But the necklace pulled tighter again, sharper this time, almost burning. His throat closed. He ripped the mask away, trembling. Shame flooded him, not only for the failures the mask denied, but for the lie he had been willing to wear.

He staggered back, clutching the rope.

The Mask Maker's voice was steady. "Masks demand habits of pretending. Wear them long enough, and the pretending becomes the pattern. You forget the truth of your own skin."

Another mask called to him, this one gold, gleaming,

and lined with jewels. He raised it and felt, suddenly, like his friends: the ones with perfect families in photos, the ones with beach houses and easy laughter. He saw himself admired, envied, finally equal. He saw gatherings where no one pitied him, where no one whispered, *What happened to Elias?*

The vision tightened around him, just as the necklace like a noose. The mask sealed against his skin, its edges fusing, making it hard to breathe. Panic clawed at his chest. He yanked at it, scraping his skin as he tore it free. His breath came ragged, his hands shaking. The mask clattered back onto the table.

The figure behind the stall tilted their head. "Masks are useful," they murmured. "They shield you, win you love, respect, belonging. But wear them too long, and, well…" their voice trailed off.

Elias's gaze drifted lower. He saw another mask, plain, carved from wood, heavy in his hands. When he slipped it on, he felt himself become *The Carer*. Always available, always responsible, carrying others' weight without question. He remembered nights when he had stayed late at his parents' house, fixing things, listening, giving. He remembered how much he had bent for his wife's needs, even when he had nothing left to give.

At first, the mask warmed him with the satisfaction of being needed, of being called dependable. But soon it grew unbearably heavy. His back bowed. His breath grew shallow. He felt crushed beneath it, swallowed by a duty that never asked what he needed in return. He pulled it off with a sob.

And then he found another, simpler still, almost forgotten in the corner. *The Friend.* He slid it over his face. Memories crowded in: long conversations at bars, picking up the phone at midnight, being there for people who leaned on him again and again. At first, it felt good. Loyal. Noble.

But slowly the mask turned cold. He remembered when he needed them but the phone never rang. When he asked for help, and silence answered. The mask pressed harder and harder, as though demanding he smile while being emptied out. He ripped it off, anger mixing with grief.

Elias staggered back. His hands shook. Around him, the masks seemed to lean forward, their painted eyes gleaming hungrily. He realised, with horror, how many of them he had worn, not just once, but for years at a time.

His father's expectations. His friends' illusions. The world's endless demands. He had been a man of masks for so long that he struggled to remember the face beneath.

His throat tightened. "I've lived my life for everyone else," he whispered. "For their eyes. Their praise. Their approval. And I don't even know who I am without it."

The Mask Maker's featureless face tilted, the white mask catching the dim light. "Habits bind you.

Masks fasten them in place. But you need not keep them. Choose bare skin. Choose your face."

Elias pressed a hand to his pocket. The compass was warm, steady. He thought of the strands of passion he had chosen, those of art, music, and teaching, with none of them requiring masks, only honesty. He thought of love, peace, freedom, all impossible to grasp with a false face.

He drew a ragged breath. "I will not wear them."

The Mask Maker raised a hand, palm open. "Then walk uncovered. It will be harder. You will feel exposed. But it will be real. And in time, the rope will loosen. Old knots will soften. New ones may be tied, not of lies, but of truth."

Slowly, Elias stepped back from the stall. The masks seemed to watch him hungrily, whispering their offers of comfort and safety. But he turned his back on them.

As he walked away, he felt the phantom weight of masks peeling from him, falling like dust. Each step away was the loosening of a knot. The air touched his bare face, cool and sharp. For the first time in years, he felt it was truly his own.

THE BRIDGE
KEEPER

The marketplace thinned until only silence stretched ahead. Elias followed a narrow lane that sloped downward, the lanterns growing fewer, their light swallowed by shadows. He walked with his compass steady in his pocket, the threads of passion warm in memory, his face bare at last. Yet a weight pressed in on him, not the burden of bundles, but the knowledge that something still waited.

The lane ended at a river. Its waters were black and restless in the darkness, rushing beneath a stone bridge. The current foamed with strange colors, flashes of gold, silver, crimson, like the remnants of lives carried downstream. The air smelled of iron and rain.

At the foot of the bridge stood the Keeper. He was tall, cloaked in grey, his face half-hidden by a hood. His hands gripped a staff carved with symbols Elias did not understand. His eyes, when they lifted, were dark as the river and just as deep.

"You have walked far, Elias," the Keeper said. His voice was low, heavy with finality. "But this is the crossing. Beyond this bridge lies not another stall, not another bargain, but the path that will carry you onward. You may not return once you set foot across. To cross, you must answer."

Elias's chest tightened. "Answer what?"

The Keeper raised his staff and pointed at the river. The waters surged, and visions rose from their depths, fragments of Elias's life, glowing, shifting, colliding.

He saw the Time Merchant's hourglass, grains frozen mid-fall.

He saw the Money Changer's golden handcuffs, glinting with hunger.

He saw the mirrors, rippling with *what might have been*.

He saw the bundles he had carried and set down.

He saw the compass, its needle steady.

He saw the threads of passion, woven and unwoven.

He saw the rope at his neck, knotted tight.

He saw the masks, row upon row, whispering lies.

The Keeper's voice rumbled. "Tell me, Elias. What have you learned?"

Elias's breath shook. The river hissed louder, as if demanding an answer.

He looked at the visions, each one aching, each one

tempting. "I learned that time cannot be bought," he said slowly. "That every grain that falls is precious because it cannot be held."

The river swirled. The hourglass sank.

"I learned that wealth can bind as much as it can free. That golden chains are still chains."

The handcuffs dissolved into the current.

"I learned that regret is endless, that every choice means the loss of another. That longing for the past steals the only life left."

The mirrors cracked, their shards swept away.

"I learned that not all burdens must be carried. That strength is in choosing which to bear, and which to lay down."

The bundles untied, their cloth floating down-stream.

He pressed a hand to his pocket. "I learned that my compass must be my own, not my father's, not my friends'. That love, peace, and freedom are my true north."

The compass gleamed bright before sinking into the waters.

His throat tightened. "I learned that passions are never lost, only neglected. That even in midlife, I can weave them back into the cloth of my days."

The threads glowed before dissolving like sparks.

Elias gripped the rope around his neck. "I learned

that habits hold more power than wishes. They can choke, blind, and lead me in circles. But if I untie the knots with patience and tie new ones with care, they can carry me where I need to go."

The necklace warmed, and for the first time, one knot loosened.

"And I learned that masks may protect, but they smother. That to live for others' eyes is to forget my own."

The masks dissolved, their painted faces melting into the current.

The river calmed. The Keeper lowered his staff. "And who are you, Elias, without all these things?"

The question struck deep. Elias's chest hollowed. Who was he, truly? Not the man of success he had tried to be. Not the father who failed or the husband who lost. Not the boy who once dreamed of guitars and pencils. He was not only his regrets, his burdens, his roles, or his wounds.

He was himself, flawed, scarred, still searching, but alive.

"I am Elias," he said. His voice shook, but it did not break. "And I will live as myself, not as anyone else's shadow."

The Keeper's eyes softened. He stepped aside. "Then cross."

Elias placed a foot on the stone bridge. The air grew sharp and clean, the sound of the river fading. Each step felt like leaving something behind: the illusions of wealth, the hunger of regret, the heaviness of masks. Halfway across, he felt lighter, though no less human. At the far end, he paused.

He looked back once. The Keeper stood silent. The river rushed on, carrying his old lessons into the depths. Elias touched the compass in his pocket, steady and warm. He stepped off the bridge.

The marketplace was gone. Ahead stretched a vast plain under a wide sky, open and waiting.

For the first time in years, Elias did not feel lost. He felt ready.

THE DAWN
TELLER

The plain unrolled before Elias like a sheet of pale cloth, the horizon stitched in the thinnest line of silver. He felt the space around him open, no more stalls, no bargaining voices, no shadows pressing close. Wind combed the grasses in one long breath. Somewhere far off a lark tried a few notes and fell quiet, as if the day had not yet decided whether to begin.

He walked until the ground sloped gently into a shallow, bowl-shaped hollow. In its center stood a low hut made of wattle and reed, roof thatched with tawny grass. No smoke rose from it. No door marked an entrance. Instead, on the side facing east, a wide arch opened like a mouth waiting to drink the sky.

Elias hesitated at the threshold.

Inside, the floor was hard-packed earth, swept clean. Shelves of driftwood lined the curved walls, each holding simple objects arranged with reverence: a clay cup the color of wet sand, a bundle of reeds bound with twine, a smooth river stone, a bell small as a walnut, a folded square of linen the pale pink of a seashell. On the far wall, a thin slit had been cut so that when the first light of the horizon came, it would pass straight through like a blade of gold.

A figure sat cross-legged in the dust, neither young nor old, hair the gray of morning fog. Their clothes were plain, their hands resting palm-up on their knees. They did not look up when Elias entered, but he felt the room acknowledge him, the way a lake acknowledges a stone that has just been thrown by widening its silence.

"Welcome," the figure said at last. Their voice was softer than thread. "You have crossed."

Elias nodded. "I have."

"Then you are ready to learn how to begin."

"I've been beginning all my life," Elias said, with a half-broken smile. "And ending."

The figure's lips tilted, not quite a smile. "You have been *continuing*. Beginning is different."

They gestured to the open arch, where the sky was lightening by degrees, as if some patient hand were washing its surface with milk.

"I am the one who tends the edge of day," they said. "I keep the hinge oiled. I ring what needs ringing so the morning swings open. Some call me the Dawn Teller. Others, the Keeper of Firsts."

Elias glanced around the hut. "You...tell the dawn?"

"I listen to it," the figure said. "And pass on what it asks."

They rose in one unhurried motion and crossed to the shelves. From the top they took the small bell and set it in Elias's palm. It was cool and surprisingly heavy. "Every morning is a door," they said. "You may stumble through it half-asleep, or you may open it. This bell is for opening."

Elias turned it gently. The metal caught a sliver of the paling sky. "If I ring it...what happens?"

"You wake," the Dawn Teller said. "Not from sleep. From habit."

They set the clay cup beside the bell. "Fill this with water at first light."

"For drinking?"

"For *promising*," they said. "Water remembers. Speak into it: one thing to *notice* today, one thing to *release*, one thing to *make*. Then drink, and let your body carry what you have chosen. Each day, choose them, and each day you tie a new knot in your rope, not one that chokes, but one that sustains."

Elias ran a thumb along the cup's rim. It was slightly uneven, a human edge. "One to notice. One to release. One to make."

"Small promises," the Dawn Teller said. "Dawn keeps only small vows. Large vows break before noon."

They lifted the cup. "Notice. Drink in what is good: a child's laughter, a moment of silence, a breath of clean air. Habits are born of attention. Tie the knot of noticing."

They rang the bell, its chime pure and fading. "Release. Let go of what no longer serves: anger, envy, comparisons. Habits are fed by what we cling to. Untie one knot, and the rope loosens."

The Dawn Teller took from a shelf on the wall, a river stone and placed it in Elias' other hand. It fit his palm as if it had waited for it. "For your pocket. It is the weight of now. When your mind rushes ahead or runs backward, place your hand on it and ask: 'Where are my feet?' If your feet are in the past or the future, return them."

Elias laughed softly, surprised by the sound of it in the bare room. "I've spent years with my feet elsewhere."

"We all have," they said, not unkindly.

They took the bundle of reeds next, untied it, and handed him a single stalk. "When you forget to breathe, put this between your teeth. The reed will make you ridiculous. Ridiculous things save lives."

"I don't understand."

"Try worrying with a reed in your mouth," the Dawn Teller said. "It makes worry shy."

Elias tucked the reed behind his ear, and the child he had once been, who sketched creatures and maps, stirred and smiled.

Outside, the horizon shivered, a faint thread brightening. The Dawn Teller went to the slit in the wall, stood with their hands at their sides, and breathed as the light inched its way in. It found the dust first, tiny constellations blooming, a galaxy at ankle height, then licked the edge of the bell in Elias's palm until the metal glowed.

"Every day will ask you a different question," the Dawn Teller said, their voice barely above the hush of wind. "Do not answer with yesterday's mouth."

"What if I don't hear the question?" Elias asked.

"You will," they said. "But you must be quiet enough to know the shape of silence."

They turned back to the shelves, lifted the pale linen square, and unfolded it across their hands. In the soft light, Elias saw that it was not plain; a faint pattern ran through it, almost too subtle to notice: lines crossing lines, a gentle grid.

"A map?" he asked.

"A cloth," they said. "But yes, also a map. Lay it on your table each morning. Place the cup at its center. Set the stone on the left, the bell on the right. Put your hands on the cloth and remind yourself: 'I stand here.' Then choose your three small vows. Say them into the water. Drink. Ring. Begin."

"And if I fail?"

"You will," the Dawn Teller said simply. "Begin again.

Dawn is not a judge. It is an opening."

The thought loosened something tight behind his ribs. "I have spent so long failing loudly," he said. "And beginning only by accident."

"Then fail quietly," they said, with a warmth that might have been humor. "And begin on purpose."

The slit of light had widened into a blade now, cutting the hut cleanly in two. Dust motes sailed through it like slow snow. The Dawn Teller stepped into the bright strip and closed their eyes, face lifted, drinking the first warmth of day as if it were a broth.

"May I ask you something?" Elias said.

"You may ask many things."

"Why small vows? Why not…change everything?"

"Because you are not a market," they said. "You are a garden. Markets transform with noise and money. Gardens change with water and time."

Elias held the cup, the bell, the stone, feeling foolish and reverent at once. "What if I choose the wrong things to notice, release, or make?"

"Then tomorrow you will choose better," they said. "Notice your choosing. That is already the making of a life."

He thought of his daughter. He imagined placing her name in the cup, not as a task but as the thing to notice. He imagined releasing a particular guilt, not all guilt, just the strand that had cut deepest the day before. He imagined making one small thing, maybe a sketch; a phone call; a simple meal he could carry to someone who needed it. Love, peace, freedom, the compass words, did not feel remote here. They felt like ingredients.

The lark outside tried another string of notes. This time the day answered.

"Come," the Dawn Teller said. They led him to the arch, where the plain had begun to glow. The eastern rim reddened like a coal. "Ring."

Elias raised the bell. He hesitated, not out of doubt, but because he understood suddenly that sound can be a kind of promise. He shook his wrist gently. The bell gave a clear, bright tone, no richer than a teaspoon on china, yet it threaded the air to the far grasses and came back to him carrying distance inside it.

The Dawn Teller listened, satisfied. "Good. That is enough."

They guided him to a shallow basin near the arch where a thin trickle of water gathered from a stone spout. He filled the cup and looked into it. His own face stared back, softened by ripples.

"What will you notice?" the Dawn Teller asked.

"My daughter's voice," he said. "Even if it is only on a message."

"What will you release?"

"The urge to prove myself to ghosts."

"What will you make?"

"A first sketch," he said, surprised by the steadiness of the answer. "Bad if it must be."

"Perfect," they said, meaning *exactly enough*, not *flawless*.

He lifted the cup and drank. The water was cool, faintly mineral, as if it had passed patiently through stone for years before arriving here. He felt it lodge under his breastbone like a smooth pebble.

The Dawn Teller took nothing back. They did not ask for payment. They merely handed him the folded cloth and nodded toward the open land.

"One more thing," they said. From a small hook by the arch, they took a thread the color of early light, neither gold nor pink, but the blush between. They tied it lightly around Elias's wrist. "This will not hold you to anything. It only reminds. When you see it, ask: 'What door am I opening right now?' If none, find a knob."

Elias laughed a sound like the first time a door swings without sticking. "And if the door is the wrong one?"

"Then you will know sooner," they said. "And turn the handle the other way."

They stepped back into the hut's dimness, already part of its quiet. Elias stood in the arch with the day lifting around him. He did not feel triumphant. He felt something gentler and more durable: permission.

He tucked the cloth inside his coat. The bell went into one pocket, the stone into the other. The cup he carried in his hand because it felt right to begin with an empty thing.

When he started across the plain, the sun broke the horizon, a slow coin rising out of a well. The light did not crash down. It advanced on the world with courtesy, blessing each blade of grass in order. Elias walked into it. Somewhere behind, in the hut with no door, the Dawn Teller would be laying the cloth, placing the cup, setting the bell and stone in their positions, tending the hinge of another day for someone else who needed it.

He lifted his wrist and looked at the thread. It was almost invisible in full sun, but it held the memory of first light. He touched the stone in his pocket. He felt for the compass with his other hand; its needle was steady, pointed not to a destination but to a way of moving.

"Begin," he said aloud, and the word did not echo. It absorbed.

He began.

EPILOGUE

THE RETURN

As Elias walked, the plain stretched wide beneath the rising sun, the grasses bending in a single direction, as though the whole earth were breathing. Elias walked steadily now, the compass warm in his pocket, the stone solid in his hand, the knots loose around his neck, the thread of dawn brushing his wrist when he moved.

For a long time he walked in silence. The marketplace was gone, there were no stalls, no merchants, no Keeper at the bridge, yet each of them walked with him still.

He heard the Time Merchant's dry voice: *Time cannot be owned, only lived.*

He felt again the golden handcuffs of the Money Changer and the weight of his own near-surrender.

He remembered the ache of the mirrors, showing what might have been, and the clarity that followed: regret steals more than it restores.

He carried the strength of the Weight Keeper's lesson: not every burden must be borne.

The compass in his pocket reminded him of love, peace, and freedom, his own true north.

The Weaver's threads still shimmered in memory, urging him to reclaim art, music, teaching, however humbly.

The rope warmed gently against his chest.

The masks lay behind him, their painted lies abandoned.

And the Dawn Teller's quiet promise remained: every day, a new beginning, made of small vows.

For the first time, the pieces no longer felt separate. They fitted together like stones in a wall, forming something strong enough to stand on.

Elias stopped at the crest of a hill. The land fell away into a valley dotted with small houses, fields, a road curling like a ribbon of earth. Smoke lifted from chimneys. Somewhere down there, people were waking, not to visions, not to riddles, but to lives of bills and breakfast, chores and arguments, small joys and heavy days.

He smiled faintly. The marketplace had given him truths, but here was the greater truth: life was not a fable. It was messy, demanding, and beautiful in its ordinariness.

He touched the compass in his pocket. "Success isn't money," he murmured. "But money matters, too." He thought of rent, groceries, the simple security of heat in winter. He could not live on air and ideals alone. But wealth, he saw now, was not the measure of a man. Money was a tool, not a crown. It could pay bills, open doors, buy time to sketch or play a guitar, but it could not replace love, nor quiet a restless spirit.

He breathed deep. For so long he had lived as though only great achievements counted. But the revelation was quieter: happiness lay in choosing with care, in honoring small promises, in weaving passion into days that still carried weight.

Suddenly and without malice, the ground tilted and he staggered forward, reaching out blindly as the world folded around him.

When he opened his eyes, he was sitting on a wooden bench by the river in his own city. The sky above was the same pale wash of morning, the water carrying its slow burden downstream. For a heartbeat he panicked. Had he only dreamed it all?

But then he looked down. Around his wrist, the faint thread of dawn still clung. In his pocket, the compass pulsed with warmth. The stone pressed solid against his palm. The knotted rope warm against his chest.

He laughed softly, the sound startling in the quiet.

His chest felt looser, lighter.

This was no village, no enchanted marketplace. It was the ordinary world he had always known: cars humming faintly on the bridge, a jogger passing with headphones, the smell of coffee drifting from a café nearby. But he no longer saw it as a prison. The everyday had its own magic, if he chose to notice.

He thought of his daughter's voice: one thing to notice.
He thought of the ghosts of failure: one thing to release.
He thought of a sketch waiting on his desk: one thing to make.

Love. Peace. Freedom.

No longer lofty abstractions, but as daily choices.

Elias rose. He walked not quickly, not with desperation, but steadily, as a man who had found his way home and for the first time in a long time, Elias felt not that he was running out of time, but that he was walking into it.

ACKNOWLEDGEMENT

This book was born from countless conversations, quiet reflections, and the stories of those who have stood at the threshold of midlife and wondered what comes next. To everyone who has shared their questions, struggles, and hopes with me, you have given this story its heartbeat.

I am grateful to the writers and thinkers who reminded me that fiction can carry wisdom, that stories can open doors where lectures cannot. Paulo Coelho, whose The Alchemist first showed me the power of allegory, stands among them.

To my family and friends, who have persisted with me as I do my thing, thank you for your love and support.

And finally, to the reader: thank you for stepping into these pages. May you find a reflection of your own journey here, and may it guide you toward the threads that matter most to you.

www.ingramcontent.com/pod-product-compliance
Lightning Source LLC
Chambersburg PA
CBHW030512130626
46549CB00007B/2954